This book is based on the TV series *Becca's Bunch*.
Becca's Bunch is created by Chris Dicker and Conor Finnegan and is produced by JAM Media.
Becca's Big Decision is based on a television script cowritten by Shane Langan,
Siân Quill, Amy Stephenson, and P. Kevin Strader.

First edition 2020

Library of Congress Catalog Card Number pending
ISBN 978-0-7636-9247-6

19 20 21 22 23 24 CCP 10 9 8 7 6 5 4 3 2 1

Printed in Shenzhen, Guangdong, China

This book was typeset in Vision.
The illustrations were created digitally.

Candlewick Entertainment
an imprint of
Candlewick Press
99 Dover Street
Somerville, Massachusetts 02144

visit us at www.candlewick.com

Becca's Big Decision

CANDLEWICK
ENTERTAINMENT

It was morning in the clubhouse, and MJ was delivering the mail.

"Special delivery for Becca!" he said.

"Is this what I think it is?" asked Becca. She opened the envelope. "It is! I won the tickets! We get to see the Firefly Flyby from Uncle Ned's balloon."

Then she looked again. She turned the envelope upside down and shook it. "Oh, no. There are only three tickets, and there are four of us."

Becca looked at MJ. "How will I choose which one of my friends doesn't go?"

"Go and talk to the Bunch," he said. "Write down your thoughts. Then you'll know what to do."

Becca picked up the phone. "Hey, Bunch, who wants to do something fun today?" she said. "And, well — it's okay to say no."

"I say yes!" said Sylvia.

"Count me in," said Pedro.

"Do I want to do something fun?" asked Russell.

"Do bears sleep in the woods?"

"What's the fun thing we're going to do?" asked Sylvia.

"It's a surprise," Becca said. "Adventure's calling!"

Becca arrived at Russell's house. Russell was doing what he loved best — having a snack.

"I'm making acorn smoothies!" he said. "Whatever the adventure is, we're going to need snacks. Let's make an extra batch together!"

Becca wrote in her notebook.

Russell
He makes everything so much fun!

Becca and Russell went to find Sylvia.

"Hi, Sylvia. What are you doing?" asked Becca.

"I'm nearly ready — just packing my bag." She tossed in ropes, floaties, and binoculars.

"You've got everything but the kitchen sink!" said Russell.

"I can bring that, too!" said Sylvia.

Becca made a note.

Sylvia
She's ready for anything and everything!

Becca, Russell, and Sylvia went to Pedro's house.

"Pedro! What's new?"

"I'm brushing up on my first-aid skills. You never know when they might come in handy," he said. "Would you like me to show you what I've learned?"

"Yes, please!" said Russell. Pedro practiced his first-aid skills on everyone.

Becca unwrapped her wing from its bandage and wrote.

The Bunch made their way to the meadow.

"I can't wait to see what the surprise is!" said Russell.

Becca walked slowly. She still didn't know what to do.

"Have you made your decision?" MJ asked.

"I can't choose," said Becca. "It's impossible!"

"Nothing is impossible. You taught me that!" said MJ. "What have you discovered about your friends?"

Becca showed MJ her notes.

Russell puts the fun in funtastic. He has to come!

And Sylvia is always ready for any adventure.

And Pedro knows so much about, well — everything.

There was a loud *SWOOSH* as Uncle Ned appeared in his hot-air balloon.

"It's the Firefly Flyby balloon ride with Uncle Ned!" cried Pedro.

"Macadamia!" said Russell.

"Becca, you won the tickets!" said Sylvia.

"Which three are coming on board?" Uncle Ned called.

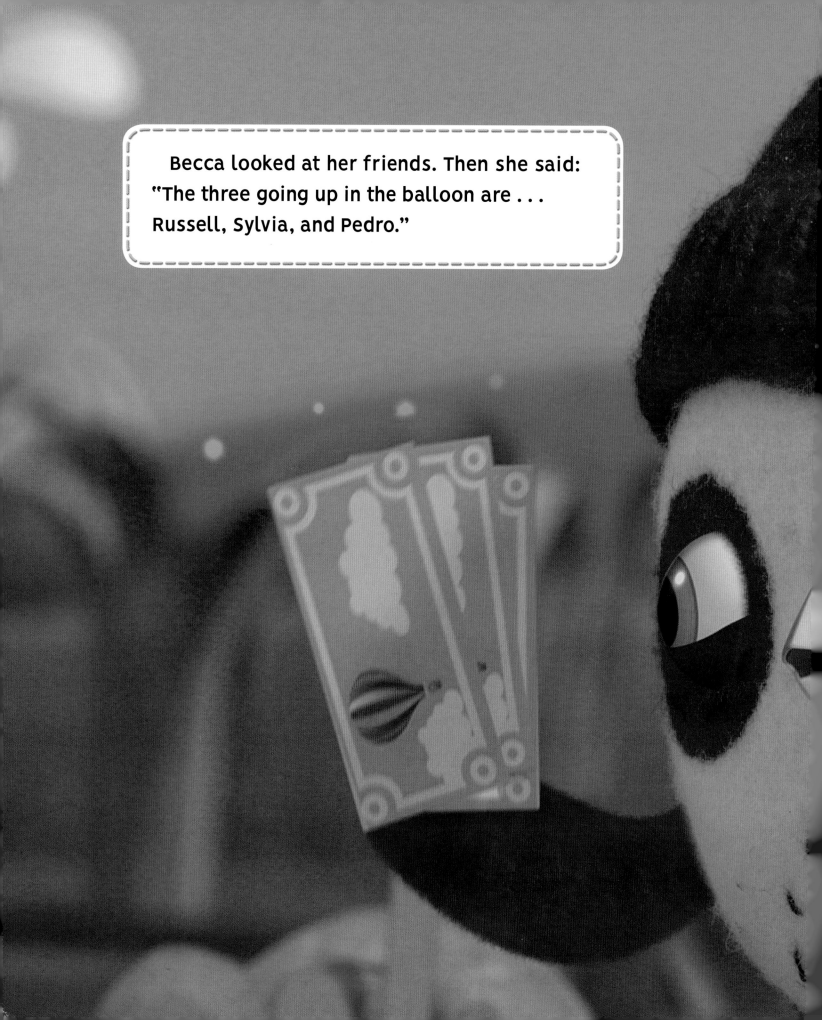

Becca looked at her friends. Then she said:
"The three going up in the balloon are . . .
Russell, Sylvia, and Pedro."

"Wait," said Sylvia. "I don't want to go without Becca."

"That goes for me, too," said Pedro.

"Me three," said Russell.

Then Uncle Ned had an idea.
"MJ, I need your help!"

Becca and the Bunch fit perfectly in the new balloon basket.

"Thanks, MJ, for letting us use your mailbag!" they called.

The Firefly Flyby was even brighter and more spectacular than the Bunch had hoped.

"All's good in the wood!" said Becca.